FLAT STANLEY's

ADVENTURES IN CLASSROOM 2E

Don't miss Flat Stanley's Worldwide Adventures!

Class Pet Surprise

Created by **Jeff Brown**
Written by **Kate Egan**
Pictures by **Nadja Sarell**

HARPER
An Imprint of HarperCollinsPublishers

Library of Congress Cataloging-in-Publication Data
Names: Egan, Kate, author. | Brown, Jeff, 1926-2003. | Sarell,
    Nadja, illustrator.
Title: Flat Stanley's adventures in classroom 2E / created by Jeff
    Brown ; written by Kate Egan ; pictures by Nadja Sarell.
Description: First edition. | New York : Harper, [2023] |
    Audience: Ages 6-10. | Audience: Grades 2-3. | Summary:
    When their second grade classroom gets a pet hamster, best
    friends Stanley and Marco disagree about building her an
    obstacle course or a maze until Stanley uses his flatness to
    make both ideas work.
Identifiers: LCCN 2022036200 | ISBN 978-0-06-309498-7
    (hardcover) | ISBN 978-0-06-309497-0 (paperback)
Subjects: CYAC: Hamsters—Fiction. | Pets—Fiction. | Schools—
    Fiction. | Best friends—Fiction. | Friendship—Fiction.
Classification: LCC PZ7.E2773 Fl 2023 | DDC [E]—dc22
LC record available at https://lccn.loc.gov/2022036200

Typography by Laura Mock
23 24 25 26 27   PC/CWR   10 9 8 7 6 5 4 3 2 1

To Mrs. Pols and the second graders
at Woolwich Central School

Contents

The Surprise

It was lunchtime at Maple Shade Elementary, and Stanley Lambchop was sitting with some kids from his second-grade class.

Stanley's best friend, Marco, unzipped his lunchbox and frowned. He took out a clear container and put it on the table. "What do you think this is?" he asked. He passed it to Stanley.

1

Stanley squinted. He could not really see inside the container. It did not look like lunch, though. It looked like a blob.

Their classmate Juniper giggled. "Is it oatmeal?" she said.

Marco shook the container, and the blob jumped up and down.

"It could be oatmeal," he said. "Or

cookie dough. Or last night's left-overs."

Marco's older sister was in charge of packing his lunch, but she did not always do a good job. She just packed whatever she found in the refrigerator. One time Marco got some cat food by mistake!

Marco held up the container and waved it in front of the other kids. "Can anyone help me solve this mystery?" he asked the whole group in a funny voice. Marco loved to make everyone laugh.

"Not me!" said a boy named Stevie, shrinking away. Many things made Stevie nervous.

"No thanks," said their classmate

Josie. She was eating soup for lunch today, and she had not spilled a single drop. Josie was very responsible.

"I'll do it!" Stanley said, laughing. "I'm brave!"

He pried the top off the container and looked inside. "Oh, it's mac and cheese!" he announced.

"Yes!" said Marco, punching the air. "It's my lucky day!"

When Marco took the first bite of his mac and cheese, Stanley took the first bite of his sandwich. Unlike his friend, he had the same lunch every day: a salami sandwich, an apple, and a juice box. Some kids might think that was boring, but Stanley Lambchop did not. Stanley had lots of adventures, after all. He did not need his lunch to be one, too.

Stanley had many adventures because he was flat. Not that long ago, a bulletin board had fallen off his bedroom wall and landed right on top of him. Now Stanley was flatter than a salami sandwich. And his flatness had made him famous! That

was why he had adventures all over the world.

When his travels were over, Stanley always liked coming back to his own house and his own school. He liked seeing his friends, of course. He liked seeing his second-grade teacher, Ms. Root, too. Ms. Root was not like any of the other teachers at school. Well, she loved science, like lots of teachers. But she also loved *surprises*! And so did Stanley Lambchop!

In fact, Ms. Root had promised her class a surprise this afternoon. "By the end of the day," she had told her class.

But the day was half over now, and they still did not know what the surprise was.

How much longer would they have to wait? Stanley wondered.

After lunch, Stanley's class had library time. They would not return to Ms. Root's room until everyone in the class had picked a book to read. Usually Stanley loved the library. Today, though, he was wishing it was already over, and it had not started yet!

As he put his lunchbox away, Stanley complained to Marco. "I'm tired of waiting to find out what the surprise is!" he said.

"I know!" Marco grumbled. "I hope it is a good surprise, not a bad surprise."

Stanley had not thought of that. "I hope the surprise is not extra homework!" he said.

Marco grinned. "I hope this surprise is not like one of my lunches!" he added.

Ms. Root's class walked in a line to the library. The kids knew what to do when they got there. They picked up their library cards and settled in on the reading rug. The library teacher, Ms. Perkinson, would read them stories before they were allowed to pick out some books.

"I wonder if Ms. Perkinson knows what the surprise is?" Stanley whispered to Marco when the other kids were settling down.

"If she does," Marco whispered back, "maybe she will give us some clues."

Stanley liked the sound of that! He paid extra attention while Ms. Perkinson was reading.

The first story she read was about a girl and her dog.

Maybe a dog was coming to visit Ms. Root's class today! Stanley thought.

But the next story was about big machines building a highway.

Was Ms. Root's class about to pave a road? Probably not, Stanley thought.

When it was time for the kids to choose their books, Stanley was still thinking about the surprise. There did not seem to be clues in Ms. Perkinson's stories. Maybe there were clues in other parts of the library?

While the rest of his class was browsing, Stanley took a look around. He went to a bookshelf in a distant corner of the library, then flattened himself against the books. When no one was watching, he peered around the shelf. Were there clues on Ms. Perkinson's desk?

No. Ms. Perkinson had a big mug of coffee on her desk. She had a laptop and a plant in a pot. But there was nothing that seemed surprising. Stanley sighed.

When Ms. Perkinson came around the corner, he unpeeled himself from the shelf. "Can I help you find a book?" she asked him.

"Oh, uh, no," Stanley stammered. "I just need another minute."

Stanley quickly picked a mystery story and checked it out with the rest of the class. Then it was time to go back to Ms. Root's room!

As he got into the line, Stanley could feel his heart beating fast. Any minute now, the class would find out what the surprise was! Stanley looked at Marco and gave him a thumbs-up.

When the class was lined up in the library, Ms. Root walked them down the hallway to their classroom. "Let's remember our manners, friends," she said as they started walking. "Let's remember to keep our voices down."

Ms. Root always called her students

"friends." Stanley did not make a peep.

Once he and his classmates settled into their seats, Ms. Root finally broke the news. "Now, I know we are all waiting for a big announcement," she said. "Who is ready to find out what our class surprise is?"

Every single student raised a hand. Stanley raised both hands at the same time and waved them!

"Friends, today I'd like to introduce you to a *new* friend," Ms. Root continued.

A new student? Stanley wondered, looking at Marco. Marco shrugged.

Then Ms. Root walked over to a closet in the corner of the classroom.

She added, "This new friend will help us in our study of science!"

Stanley was wondering why she would put a new student in a closet—and what that had to do with science—when Ms. Root opened the closet door.

Then he saw what the surprise was.

Inside the closet, there was a big glass tank.

And inside the tank, there was a hamster!

Meet Cottonball!

All at the same time, the kids in Ms. Root's class said "Oooooh!" and "Awwww!" and "It's sooooo cute!"

As Ms. Root scooped the hamster out of the tank, even Stevie leaned in to watch. For once, he did not seem afraid at all.

"Friends, I'd like you to meet Cottonball," Ms. Root announced. She walked around the room with the hamster, so everyone could see it up close.

"Cottonball comes to us from Mr. Johnson's classroom," the teacher continued. "She was living there with her sister, Cornflake. But most hamsters do not like to live with other hamsters. Mr. Johnson thinks she will be happier here with us."

The teacher kept one hand on top of Cottonball to keep her from jumping, but Stanley could still see what she looked like. Cottonball was bigger and fluffier than a mouse. She was about as long as a cell phone, with a round body and a short tail. She was mostly a sort of orange color, but her belly was white. Her whiskers were twitching.

Stanley's classmate, Elena, leaped up and moved toward Ms. Root. "Can I pet her?" she asked.

Stanley wanted to pet her, too! This was better than any surprise he had imagined. Stanley had never had a pet! Not at home, and not at school.

The teacher put her hand up like a stop sign. "Soon! But not yet," she said. "We don't really know Cotton-ball, and she does not know us, either. We don't want to frighten her." She stroked the hamster's head gently.

Once everyone had seen her, Ms. Root put Cottonball back into the tank. Then she walked to the back of the classroom and placed the tank on top of a bookshelf.

"Cottonball will not be living in the closet, of course," Ms. Root explained. "That was just for the surprise. Her new home will be right here!"

Josie raised her hand as Ms. Root put a mesh panel over the top of the tank. "Ms. Root?" she asked. "Don't hamsters live in cages?"

The teacher nodded. "That is an excellent question, Josie."

Stanley looked at Marco, who sat right next to him.

Ms. Root *always* thought Josie's questions were excellent.

"Some hamsters live in cages," the teacher explained. "But many cages are just too small. Hamsters need plenty of room to explore. This big glass tank offers Cottonball a lot more space! Would you like to see what it's like inside?"

Josie stood up and walked over to the tank. The whole class followed, crowding around her. Stanley and Marco were stuck in the back of the pack. They could barely see a thing.

Sometimes, Stanley thought, being flat was very handy. He slipped through a small space between two girls, Juniper and Sophia, and pulled Marco past Sophia's wheelchair. Pretty soon, he and Marco were right in the front row of kids, looking into Cottonball's glass house!

The hamster was burrowing into a big pile of wood shavings. Stanley could see her tiny feet digging, and her tiny ears sticking out of the heap. When she stopped for a second, she caught Stanley's eye.

Meanwhile, Ms. Root pointed out the highlights of Cottonball's home.

"There's an upstairs and a downstairs, see?" she said. "Connected by this ramp." The ramp was made of light wood, and it led to a platform.

"Her food bowl is right here," said Ms. Root, pointing to what looked like the world's tiniest cereal bowl beneath the platform. "But Cottonball likes to store her food in other places. We will probably find some in her bed!"

Sophia laughed. "And she doesn't even get in trouble? In my family, we can only eat snacks in the kitchen."

There was a round thing near the food bowl, Stanley noticed. It looked almost like the Ferris wheel he had ridden at a theme park last summer, but much smaller.

"What's that?" he asked, pointing.

"Cottonball loves to run on that wheel," Ms. Root said. "That is how she gets her exercise. It is like a treadmill for hamsters."

Just then, Cottonball stopped digging and scampered into a little red house inside the cage.

"It looks like a little doghouse!" Stanley's classmate Evan called out.

"Or a dollhouse!" Elena added.

"Hamsters love to hide," Ms. Root told her class. "In the wild, they look for places where they can be safe and secure. But in a classroom, a hamster house is just as good!"

Stanley and Marco looked at each other again. Stanley was pretty sure Marco was thinking what he was thinking. There were wild hamsters? *Where*? They would have to find out more about this.

When Stanley turned back to the hamster house, Cottonball was peeking out! She looked at him until she scurried into a place where there were not any windows. Stanley just *knew* they were going to be friends.

"Now, class," Ms. Root went on, "Cottonball is going to teach us a great deal about animal life. We will learn from Cottonball just by observing her. Every day, we will see how hamsters live and behave." She smiled her biggest smile. This was the smile she always had when she was talking about science.

Stanley had so many questions!

He wondered what Cottonball ate and how the class was going to take care of her. Would they have to clean her tank? Would they get to play with her? What was she doing right now?

But Ms. Root wanted to give Cottonball some space. "Let's give our new friend a chance to settle in," she said. "Our class pet needs time to get used to our classroom. And we have some work to do before the end of the day."

Soon Ms. Root was writing on the board. It was time for math, and the class was playing a new game. Pairs of kids had to guess what shapes were hidden inside some cloth bags. Were they cubes, or spheres, or cylinders, or pyramids?

It would be hard to think about shapes when the class had a new pet, Stanley thought. But people with pets could not play with them all the time, he knew. Maybe Cottonball was ready for a nap.

As usual, Stanley and Marco were a team. They piled their bags on Stanley's desk. The fabric was thin and slippery, but they could not see through it. When Stanley picked up a bag, he could feel there were sharp edges inside.

"That one's definitely a pyramid!" Marco said.

"I have a sphere!" Juniper yelled from across the room.

Each pair was supposed to write down their guesses on a sheet of paper taped to the wall. Stanley was the notetaker for his team. He tried to write neatly with a marker, but the paper kept slipping around. He could hear it crinkling as he wrote.

And then Stanley could hear another sound. It was a tap-tap-tap in the back of the classroom.

Was it the radiator? Was something leaking? Once Stanley heard it, he could not tune it out.

"Do you hear that?" he asked Marco.

Marco tilted his head. "Actually . . .

yes? You mean the tapping? It's coming from . . ."

Suddenly Stanley knew just where it was coming from.

He cut in before Marco could finish. ". . . Cottonball!"

Stop That Hamster!

The boys dropped their mystery shapes and rushed to the bookshelf. They could see the mesh panel on the tank popping up and down. They could see a furry face burrowing under the panel. Then they could see the panel flying away from the shelf!

And a hamster jumping out of her tank in a flash.

"No!" cried Stanley.

"Stop that hamster!" Marco called out.

But no one else had seen what happened. The other kids were still working with their shapes at their desks.

Cottonball jumped onto some books that were sticking out of the shelf. There were enough of them that they were like a hamster staircase. Within a couple of seconds, Cottonball was on the classroom floor. And then she was off!

The class pet raced across the classroom, dodging desks and feet. She zigzagged from one side of the room to the other—from the bookshelf to the windows and back.

"Stop that hamster!" Marco said again, a little louder. Now he had everyone's attention.

Elena spotted the runaway hamster and covered her mouth with her hands. Her eyes grew huge. "She's running away!" she said. "I never even got to pet her!"

Ms. Root said, "Let's stay calm, friends," but her voice was shaking. "This is not what we expected from our first day with Cottonball. But when she gets tired of running, we will be able to catch her."

"Unless she gets to the door first!" Marco pointed out.

The classroom's door was wide open right now, opening to the hallway of

Maple Shade Elementary School. If Cottonball got out there, it would be much harder to find her. The hallway was big, and busy. She might even get hurt! After all, no one would expect to find a hamster there.

Ms. Root ran to the door. She slammed it shut just in time! Cottonball skittered to a stop in front of it and stood there for a second, blinking.

Maybe I can get her! Stanley thought. But many of his classmates had the same idea. And when five sets of hands moved toward her, Cottonball got spooked. As the class closed in on her, she spun around and sprinted to the nearest corner of the room. In no time, she was hiding

behind the trash
can.

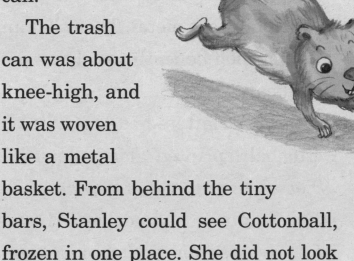

The trash
can was about
knee-high, and
it was woven
like a metal
basket. From behind the tiny
bars, Stanley could see Cottonball,
frozen in one place. She did not look
very happy.

Marco put his finger to his lips
and looked at the other kids. "Shhhh!
This is it!" he whispered. He tiptoed
toward the trash can. He would catch
Cottonball off guard!

But as he inched closer to the
hamster, she caught Marco off guard

instead. Suddenly she climbed up one side of the trash can, her little feet gripping the metal. Then she ran onto the shelf beneath the classroom whiteboard!

Markers clattered to the floor as Cottonball sprinted along the shelf. When she got to the other side, she jumped onto the windowsill. In no time, she was hiding behind a window shade.

Stanley sighed. Having a pet was not supposed to be like this.

He stood very still because he didn't want to scare the hamster again. But he also wanted to help her. He wanted her to like being their class pet!

Ms. Root picked up the cord that adjusted the shades and tied it in a knot away from Cottonball. "We want to make sure Cottonball doesn't chew anything that could hurt her," she explained.

Stanley could see a hamster tail under the shade.

"What do we do now?" asked Evan. He was breathing hard, as if he—not Cottonball—had been running all over the place.

"Maybe we can lure her out with a treat," Josie said.

"That is an excellent idea," said Ms. Root.

"Yes, Josie, that is an excellent idea," Marco echoed, nodding. He looked knowingly at Stanley.

"We don't even know what hamsters eat," Stanley pointed out.

It turned out Stevie knew, though. "My family used to have a hamster," he said. Was that why he wasn't scared of Cottonball? Stanley wondered.

Stevie added, "You can give hamsters lots of fruits and vegetables, as long as you cut them up super small."

"I have an apple from my lunch!" Stanley said. He had not eaten it at lunchtime. He had been too excited to find out the surprise!

So Stevie used a pair of classroom scissors to snip a chunk off the side of the apple, then cut the chunk into

pieces. Evan arranged them on a little sheet of paper, as if it were a plate,
and put the apple pieces close to the
window shade.

"Now we just wait," said Ms. Root.
She turned to Stanley and Marco.
"Boys, can you tell us what hap-
pened? How did Cottonball escape?"

There was no way to be sure, but
Marco had a guess. "Cottonball would
have had to climb up something to
get to the top of the tank," he said.
"Maybe it was her water bottle?"

And Stanley had noticed something else. "The mesh thing goes over
the top of the tank, right?" he asked.
"But were we supposed to lock it?" He
picked the panel up off the floor and

showed Ms. Root a latch on its side.

The teacher went pale. "Oh no," she said. "I did not know there was a lock! This is all my fault!"

Stevie tried to comfort Ms. Root. "Our hamster escaped at home, too," he said. "But we got her back! At least we know where Cottonball is. My family did not know that our hamster was hiding under our couch. I think Cottonball will be okay."

While everyone else stood by the tank, Stanley kept an eye on the window shade. Cottonball was still right behind it.

Until . . . suddenly . . . she wasn't!

Cottonball darted out and grabbed a piece of apple from the paper plate.

She nibbled at it, holding the piece of apple in her paws.

No one else was looking, and Stanley did not say a word. He did not want everyone to rush at her again.

Instead, he watched Cottonball eat her snack. He watched her dash across the windowsill, jump onto a chair, then climb down a chair leg to the floor. He watched her disappear under the radiator.

That was when Stanley Lambchop had a good idea.

He did not like the way Ms. Root's good surprise had turned into a bad surprise. Luckily, Stanley knew how to save this day! He lay down on the classroom floor and slid under the radiator. No one else would be able to do this. No one else would be able to fit!

There was not much space under the radiator. There was a lot of dust down there, along with a bunch of missing pencils. Cottonball was stuck between a pencil and a radiator pipe.

"Come here," Stanley said to the hamster. "I won't hurt you, I promise."

• Cottonball just watched. She didn't try to run away. Maybe she believed what Stanley told her! Anyway, she kept still as Stanley moved one hand slowly toward her body. When he felt her soft fur, he grabbed her.

"Sorry I'm squeezing you," he told her. "This will only take a minute." When he slid out from under the radiator, she was still in his hand.

"I got her!" he told the class. "She's safe!"

He found that he did not have to squeeze her too tight. If he just kept a hand on top of her, like Ms. Root had before, she couldn't get away.

The hamster did not squirm or seem upset. Maybe she did not mind being held, Stanley thought. Her fur was fluffy and light. Now Stanley knew why she was named Cottonball.

He petted her head gently and turned toward Ms. Root. "If they are super careful, can the other kids pet her now, too?" Stanley asked. Stanley wanted them to feel how soft she was. And he wanted Cottonball to feel like she was a member of the class!

Ms. Root nodded. "Yes, Stanley, I think this is the right time. As long as we take turns and keep our voices low. We don't want to scare her. After all, we don't want this speedy hamster to make another escape!"

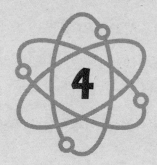

Obstacle Course

After school, Marco came home on the school bus with Stanley. The boys did not always have play dates on school days, but sometimes the Lambchop parents and the Ramirez parents helped each other out if they had things to do. Marco had an older sister who was a teenager. She babysat for other families, and she could probably babysit for Marco, too. But she was the one who packed the lunches! Marco did not want her to pick him up at school.

When they were at the Lambchops' house, Stanley and Marco always did the same things. First, they had a snack, and then they built an obstacle course. The boys would take every bit of playground equipment out of the Lambchops' shed and put it all over the yard. Then they would race through all the stations.

Today the boys were having pretzels and peanut butter for a snack. "Do hamsters like peanut butter?" Marco wondered. "Toby loves peanut butter."

Toby was Marco's dog. Unlike the

Lambchops, the Ramirezes had a lot
of pets. Two cats, a rabbit, a dog, and
a parakeet. They even had a lizard!

Stanley shook his head. "I'm not
sure if hamsters like peanut butter,"
he said. "But I don't think Cottonball
can have it at school, anyway."

Marco thought about that as he reached for another pretzel. "I guess you're right," he said. "If we can't have it, why would she?" Peanut butter was not allowed at Maple Shade Elementary because of allergies.

"Speaking of Cottonball," Marco added, "I can't believe you caught her!"

Stanley smiled modestly. He was proud of his quick thinking. "Why do you think she ran away?" he asked Marco.

Marco shrugged. "Maybe she wanted to see our classroom or something. After all, it's a lot more exciting than Mr. Johnson's room!" Mr. Johnson's class had to keep their desks in straight lines. They were always singing a cleanup song, even in the middle of the day.

"Well, next time we can show her around," Stanley said. "I don't think she should be exploring on her own." It was way too easy for a hamster to get lost at school, he thought.

Marco drank a whole glass of milk and stood up from the table. "Ready?" he asked.

Stanley nodded. He was definitely ready. They had an obstacle course to build!

Today the boys hauled a mini-trampoline out of the shed, along with a gymnastics mat, a ring-toss set, and a Frisbee. It took a long time to arrange them all in the yard.

The trampoline went on the edge of the grass, near the back fence. The gymnastics mat went in the middle of the lawn, between the trampoline and the Lambchops' swing set. Then, on the other side of the swing set, the boys placed the ring toss and the Frisbee.

"I've got it!" Stanley said. "Listen to this!" He could see the whole obstacle course in his head already. "Ten jumps on the trampoline, and then jump off and onto the mat."

"Right!" said Marco. "And how about a front flip and a backflip once we get there?" Both boys loved to do somersaults.

"Great!" said Stanley. "Then a twist on the swing . . ." He did not have to explain any more to Marco. Marco knew that meant sitting down, spinning the swing around till the chains were all twisted up, then spinning back superfast.

"Get all three rings on the ring toss," Marco added. There was one wooden peg for all the rings.

"And then toss the Frisbee over the finish line!" Stanley finished for him. Stanley and Marco were always finishing each other's sentences. That was one way people could tell they were best friends.

Stanley took a deep breath. "Okay, then," he said. "Ready to get started?"

The boys set a timer and tried out the obstacle course!

Marco went first. He jumped so fast on the trampoline that Stanley lost count of his jumps, but he stalled out on the ring toss. It was pretty hard to get the rings on the peg! When he finished the whole course, Stanley showed him his time. Marco just shook his head.

"That stinks!" he said. "I know I can beat that next time!"

When it was Stanley's turn, he had to take a break after the swing spin. He was so dizzy that he couldn't walk straight! There was no way he could do the ring toss until the world stopped whirling around him. "My time stinks, too!" he said when he was finally finished. His flatness did not help him on the obstacle course at all.

After they each went through the course a couple of times, they got a little faster. They moved more smoothly between the different parts, too.

Then, by mistake, Marco threw a ring instead of the Frisbee! It flew toward the Lambchops' house and landed on the back stairs. That was not supposed to happen!

The boys were both laughing when Stanley's mom came out onto the porch. "Marco, your dad will be here for pickup soon," Mrs. Lambchop said.

Stanley and Marco dragged the trampoline and the mat back to the shed. They put away the rings and the Frisbee. Then they flopped onto the grass to rest before Marco had to leave.

"I'm so tired!" Stanley said. His muscles were aching.

"Me too!" said Marco. He stuck his tongue out, like he was panting. "But you know what people always say at dog training?"

"What?" Stanley asked.

"People say 'A tired dog is a good dog,'" Marco said. "That is what my family learned with Toby. He won't chew things or bark as much if he is all worn out."

Stanley laughed. "So we will be good kids because we are tired kids?" he asked.

Marco nodded. "I bet that's what grown-ups think," he said. "Maybe they think we will go to bed early. Or help with the dishes or something."

For some reason that reminded Stanley of Cottonball.

Ms. Root had said Cottonball got exercise on her wheel. It was like a hamster treadmill.

But what if that was not enough? Stanley wondered. Actually, he thought, what if that was why she ran away?

He sat up straight. "Marco, what if

a tired hamster is a good hamster?" Stanley asked.

"Um, yeah, maybe," Marco said. "That makes sense . . ."

"And a not-tired hamster can get into trouble," Stanley added.

He kept on talking. "I mean, what if that is why she climbed out of her cage? Maybe she wasn't running away," he said. "Maybe she just needed to burn up some energy. Like we do at recess."

"I bet wild hamsters get lots of exercise," Marco joked.

Stanley grinned. He still couldn't believe there were wild hamsters. He had never heard of a hamster outside a pet store. But that thought was suddenly crowded out by another good idea.

"Maybe Cottonball would like to get *more* exercise," he said. He walked around the yard as the idea took shape.

"We don't want the hamster to run around the classroom again," said Marco. "You heard what Stevie said. We were lucky that we found her!"

Stanley had something different in mind, though. He knew Cottonball would not be safe in their classroom, or on the playground. But what if she had a hamster playground?

He flopped down next to Marco

again, just as Marco was getting up. The boys' eyes met, then their minds met.

Then, at the same time, they both said the same thing. "She needs an obstacle course of her own!"

Design Time

Stanley could hardly wait to tell Ms. Root all about it. But when he arrived at school the next day, the class had some important jobs to do first. "I need somebody to refill Cottonball's food bowl," Ms. Root said. "Would anyone like to volunteer? Oh, yes, thank you, Josie."

Other people put their hands up to give Cottonball some fresh water

and a little bit of hay. Someone even volunteered to scoop out the corner of the tank that Cottonball used as a bathroom!

"It's all part of learning about hamsters," Ms. Root said. "This is living science!"

Once Stanley's classmates had

returned to their seats, Ms. Root had a question. "Does anyone notice anything different about Cottonball's cage today?" she asked.

Elena and Evan both waved their hands in the air. "I noticed something!" Elena said. "It looked like Cottonball was making a tunnel in her wood shavings!"

"Yes!" said Ms. Root. "That is something hamsters like to do! In the wild, they know they can be safe in a tunnel."

Stanley did not dare to look at Marco. Wild hamsters again!

"And they can also use tunnels to travel without being seen," Ms. Root went on. "Did you know that hamsters can go a long way? They can travel up to five miles in one day!"

Juniper spoke without being called on. "I don't think I could walk five miles in a day. And I'm a lot bigger than a hamster!"

"See?" Stanley whispered to Marco. "I bet it's boring to run so far on that wheel."

The boys had to wait until reading time to share their big idea with Ms. Root. When everyone else was reading with a buddy, Stanley and Marco walked to the front of the classroom together.

"Ms. Root, guess what?" Stanley asked her.

Ms. Root smiled. She tilted her

head and threw her hands up in the air. "I give up, Stanley!" she said. "What is it?"

"We have a surprise for you!" Marco jumped in.

Ms. Root's eyes lit up, just as both boys had expected. "A surprise?" she asked.

"Yes!" Stanley and Marco said at the same time. "And it is better than a regular surprise. It is a *scientific* surprise!"

Ms. Root clapped her hands together. "Science and surprises! Two of my favorite things! Well, when are you going to tell me what it is?"

Stanley stood up straight, even though that made him stretch out like something that had been wrapped too tight. He would speak for both of them, since it was his idea.

"It is a plan to help Cottonball," he said with pride. "We know she needs exercise, right? Just like most kids. But unlike most kids, she does not have a lot of ways to get it. So Marco and I want to build her an obstacle course!"

"Kind of like a playground," Marco added.

"It will have many different fun activities!" Stanley exclaimed.

Ms. Root looked like someone had just given her a birthday present with a bow on top. "What a wonderful surprise!" she said. "It is science plus science! You will take what you are learning about hamsters and add a little engineering!"

Stanley beamed at Marco. He stood up even straighter, if that was possible. Science plus science sounded good to him. So did engineering, whatever that was.

When the class went to library that afternoon, Ms. Root made sure that Ms. Perkinson knew what they were planning. "These boys have big ideas," the teacher said to the librarian. "Do you have any books about engineering projects?"

In no time, Stanley and Marco were sitting at a library table with a stack of books. Stanley didn't see what they needed, though. The books were for kids who were entering science fairs, or kids who wanted to build forts, or kids who wanted to take things apart and put them back together again.

"I wish there was a book about building for hamsters!" Stanley complained to Marco.

But Stanley sort of knew what he wanted already. He wanted to make something that would be fun and a challenge for Cottonball, all at the same time. Different activities would keep her interested. Going around and around on a hamster wheel was like only ever going on the swings, Stanley thought, and never on the slide.

So he started to draw a picture of what was in his mind. Marco was still looking at the books when Stanley took out a pencil and a piece of paper.

Cottonball was a good jumper, he remembered. So there should be something for her to jump on. A trampoline, he thought at first. Only he could not really picture a hamster on a trampoline. So what if it was just a thing to jump over? Or through? Like a hoop?

He drew a picture and nudged his friend. "Hey, check this out!" he said. But Marco was looking at a book of games and puzzles, like mazes and crosswords.

Stanley giggled. "Hamsters can't do puzzles," he pointed out. "Come help me over here!" He was already adding something to his sketch.

Cottonball was also great at climbing, Stanley knew. He had seen her climb out of the tank and into trouble! So maybe there should be something for climbing, he thought. A ladder would be good. But a ladder to where?

He chewed the end of his pencil and thought for a while. Instead of a ladder, he realized, maybe he could make a little bridge. Just an archway she could climb up and over. It was perfect!

"Hey Marco, look at this!" said

Stanley, pointing at his sketch.

"Hey, Stanley, look at this!" said Marco. He was working on a sketch of his own now.

"Just hang on a second . . ." Stanley replied. He turned back to his paper. Stanley Lambchop was on a roll.

He asked himself questions as he looked for new ideas. What else would the hamster enjoy? Well, what other fun things were on playgrounds for kids?

Stanley and his younger brother, Arthur, loved to seesaw. The school playground did not have a seesaw, but a different playground in their town did. It was the brothers' favorite thing to play on! Of course, Cottonball did not have a brother or a best friend to seesaw with, Stanley remembered. But she could hop on one end, and then run around to hop on the other. She might like to watch it go up and down, or stand in the middle to make it balance. Perfect!

Stanley stood up and stretched. "We just need one more thing now," he said.

He was talking to Marco, but Marco was not there. Was he off with the rest of the class? Stanley wondered.

Oh well, he thought. He could finish the sketch by himself. He already knew that there would be a snack at the end of the obstacle course. All kids liked snacks after playing, and he'd bet hamsters did, too!

Stanley stood back to look at his plan. This obstacle course would solve two problems for Cottonball. She would have a lot more exercise— and a lot more fun! The class hamster was going to love it.

But where was Marco? When Stanley finally found him sitting in a beanbag chair, Marco was distracted.

"I have it all worked out!" Stanley said. He waved his sketch at Marco to get his friend's attention. "This will be the best obstacle course any hamster ever had!"

But Marco did not finish his sentence this time. That was because

Marco had a completely different idea.

"Wait! No, I have it all worked out!" Marco said. He stood up and explained. "I was thinking we should go in another direction. Something instead of an obstacle course."

"What?" said Stanley.

"I just know Cottonball will love it!" Marco said. "I think we should build a maze!"

Building Blocks

Stanley was confused. He and Marco were supposed to be working together!

He would have to change Marco's mind. "But we said . . ." Stanley began.

"A maze is better," Marco said firmly. "Cottonball can have a different adventure every time she runs through it."

"That would happen on the obstacle

course, too!" Stanley argued. He could not believe what he was hearing.

Marco got out of the beanbag chair. He put his hands on his hips. He looked at Stanley and waited.

That was when Stanley realized he would have to make a choice.

If he wanted to work with Marco, he would not be able to work on his

obstacle course. If he wanted to work on his obstacle course, he would not be able to work with Marco. It was one way or another. And Stanley liked his own idea too much to leave it behind.

"Well, I guess we can each do our own thing," Stanley snapped.

He did not mean to snap—it just came out that way. His feelings were a little hurt.

"You don't have to be mad," Marco snapped back.

Well, now Stanley *was* mad! He had a lot of questions, too. Why did Marco change his mind about the obstacle course? Stanley wondered. Had Stanley done something wrong?

And could they still be friends? For all Stanley knew, Marco wanted to build a maze with someone else.

Stanley blinked and walked away. The class was lining up to leave the library, and Stanley was at the front of the line. He didn't talk to Marco. He didn't talk to anybody. Except for Cottonball, that is. When he walked back into Ms. Root's room, Stanley made sure to say hello to the hamster.

"Just you wait!" he told Cottonball. "My obstacle course will be the best ever!"

The class was so busy that Stanley did not have time to work on his project. But Ms. Root made an exciting offer at the end of the day. "Stanley," she said, "Would you like to stay after school to build your obstacle course? I will be working late this afternoon." She would even help him get in touch with his parents.

There was only one problem. Stanley and Marco were *both* supposed to go home to the Lambchops' after school. So now they would *both* be staying after school with Ms. Root.

Once the bell rang and the buses came, the two boys stayed with their teacher. On some other day this might have been fun, but today it was pretty awkward. Stanley made his way to the Art Corner and pretended Marco wasn't even there.

The Art Corner was the part of the classroom where Ms. Root kept the art supplies. She had every supply that anyone could ever imagine! There were the usual things like paints and markers, but also some unusual things like beads and wooden dowels and strips of cardboard. Ms. Root kept the art supplies in big bins so full they were overflowing. Stanley's mom, Mrs. Lambchop, believed in keeping everything neat and tidy. But Ms. Root believed that sometimes kids had to make a mess!

Stanley took some scissors and some cardboard from a bin, along with some popsicle sticks and glue. From the corner of her eye, Ms. Root spotted him. "All of those materials will be safe for hamsters," she told Stanley. "You're off to a good start!"

That was nice to hear. But Ms. Root told Marco the same thing! The two boys worked side by side at their desks, but they did not talk.

Stanley tried not to think about his friend. Or whether Marco even

was his friend anymore. It was time to build!

First, he cut a circle out of cardboard. Then he cut a window out of it for Cottonball to jump through. Right away, he saw had a problem. A circle could not stand! Stanley would have to find a way to prop it up.

But that was easier to imagine than to do. Stanley tried a few different ways, but the hoop fell over every time! Finally, he glued the hoop to some popsicle sticks. Then he glued those popsicle sticks to some other popsicle sticks that he laid flat on his desk. The hoop was inside a solid wooden structure. There was no way it could fall down now.

The first part of his obstacle course was done! Phew! Stanley glanced over at Marco. He wished he could show his friend what he made. But Marco was busy cutting strips of cardboard to make the lanes of his maze. He did not even look in Stanley's direction.

Ms. Root had been busy on her computer, but she went to the back of the room to check on Cottonball. Then she checked on the boys. "Marco?" she asked gently, after looking at the maze walls he was beginning to build. "Are you leaving enough room for Cottonball in there?"

Marco looked up. "What do you mean?" he asked.

"Is there enough space for a

hamster between those walls?" Ms. Root asked. She held her hands a couple of inches apart. "Cottonball is about this wide. You do not want her to get stuck!"

Uh-oh, Stanley thought. He looked at his hoop. He measured it with a ruler. The space was going to be a tight squeeze! The wooden structure was great, but it was no good if the hoop was too small.

Stanley took a deep breath. Then he made a decision. He was going to put the hoop aside for now. He would come back to it in a little while. He would build the hamster bridge instead!

Okay, Stanley thought. An arched

bridge would be hard to make with popsicle sticks. Popsicle sticks did not bend! But he could use them to build legs for each side of a bridge. Then he could stretch some paper between them. Maybe he would even paint the bridge an orangey-red color, Stanley thought, like the Golden Gate Bridge. That was a famous spot he had visited on an adventure in California. Cottonball would love it!

Stanley built one side of the bridge, a strong pillar of popsicle sticks. Then he built another one to match. But when he stretched a piece of paper between the sides, it ripped in the middle. And this was before a hamster was even walking on it!

Stanley stood up and took a step back from his bridge. A piece of paper was not going to hold a hamster. Maybe a piece of fabric would work?

He rummaged around in the Art Corner bins. He found a piece of cloth, cut it to the perfect size, and stretched it between the bridge legs. But when Stanley pulled the cloth tight, the legs leaned over. And if he kept it loose, the fabric sagged. It was more like a hammock than a bridge! It looked like a place where a hamster could take a nap.

Stanley sighed. He was feeling discouraged. His obstacle course was not working! Maybe Marco's idea was better all along.

But when he looked over at Marco, he saw something he did not expect. Marco had his head down on his desk. Was he stuck, too?

That was when Ms. Root returned. She was much more cheerful than Stanley and Marco. She was smiling, just like always.

"Boys," she said. "It looks like you've hit a rough patch. But this is all part of being an engineer!"

Stanley and Marco sighed at the same time. Then the teacher said, "Don't worry, boys, I have an idea to help!"

Trying Again

Stanley already knew that Ms. Root was a great teacher. But now he wondered if Ms. Root was a mind reader, too. Somehow she knew what he needed to learn right now. He needed to learn what it meant to be an engineer!

"Engineers are people who use science to solve problems," Ms. Root explained to Stanley and Marco.

"They invent and build new ways to do things. Some engineers make structures, some make systems, some make programs. But they all try to make life better, or easier, or maybe even more fun."

"That's what I wanted to do for Cottonball," said Stanley, "but now I am not so sure."

"That's what you *are* doing," Ms. Root said firmly, "but you have only taken the first step."

Stanley felt like he had taken *a lot* of steps! But his teacher went on. "An engineer makes plans before building, just like you did. They sketch things out as well as they can. But no engineer can predict the future. They do not know if their plans will work until they try them."

"I think I can predict the future," Marco muttered. "My maze is hopeless."

Stanley tried to hide his smile. He felt exactly the same way about his obstacle course!

Ms. Root continued. "Part of

engineering," she said, "is trying things out and testing them. Most engineers don't get everything right the first time they build something. So what do you think they do next?"

Stanley looked at the floor. "I guess they try again," he said. Not that he wanted to.

Ms. Root clapped her hands together. "Yes!" she exclaimed. "Engineers don't give up! They make adjustments! They tinker and try again!"

Marco exhaled, and his hair ruffled in the breeze. "I already did that," he reported. "And it didn't work."

Stanley had to agree. "I don't know what else to try," he told Ms. Root.

"I have some ideas," Ms. Root said. "But I also have a promise."

Stanley and Marco looked at each other, then looked away from each other. Stanley was almost forgetting he was mad. "A promise?" he asked.

"Yes," Ms. Root said. "I promise that each time you try a new solution for your problem, it will be better than the last one. If you are persistent, you will find the best way."

Stanley shrugged. "I hope so," he said. "I mean . . . I guess I can try one more time . . ." It was hard to say no to Ms. Root when she was so excited about everything. And she'd said she had ideas. If he got stuck again, she could help.

Marco went back to his maze first. Stanley could see him taking out some of the walls of his maze. Maybe he was making it simpler? Stanley thought. Cottonball would still like it, even if it was not advanced.

When Stanley looked at the hoop again, he saw a problem he could fix. Maybe he did not need ideas from Ms. Root after all. He cut out a new, bigger circle that would be the right fit for Cottonball. He built a new wooden structure. And soon he had one part of the obstacle course finished! Now Stanley was ready to move on.

The bridge was a bigger challenge. Stanley tried to connect the legs with a piece of cardboard, but

the cardboard was too hard to glue in place. It kept wiggling around on the legs! This would not be a safe bridge for Cottonball. But what else could Stanley do?

He stopped building and just stared at the bridge, frustrated. Then he had an idea. He would build a different kind of bridge!

Stanley put the legs aside and started over. He glued two popsicle sticks together so that they came to a point. Then he glued many more sticks to the first ones. Eventually he had what looked like a ramp going up, coming to a point, and another ramp going down. It was a little steep, but Cottonball could manage. Yes!

Beside him, Marco was humming as he worked on his maze. He kept tracing the possible maze paths with his finger. He did not want them to be too hard or too easy.

When Marco looked up, Stanley blurted, "I think your maze looks good." Marco grinned, and Stanley grinned back. Maybe they could be friends again, after all. Someday. This thought made Stanley happy as he went back to work.

It turned out that building a hamster seesaw was pretty simple. Stanley glued two popsicle sticks together. Then he glued a wooden dowel to the bottom, right in the middle. Stanley checked to make sure both sides of the seesaw were even. He got it right on the first try! Did that ever happen to real engineers? Stanley wondered. He hoped so!

All that was left was the snack. It would be Cottonball's reward at the end of the obstacle course. Or maybe it would be her reason for running through it in the first place? Stanley didn't know what food would work best though. Another apple, or something else?

"Ms. Root?" he called across the room. "Can I ask you something?"

"Of course!" she said cheerfully.

"What kind of snack should Cottonball get at the end of the obstacle course?" Stanley asked.

Ms. Root came over to take a look at the obstacle course. "I like that see-saw," she said. "But let's think about the snack. Should our class pet get a treat every time she plays here?"

Stanley shrugged. "Sure! Why not?"

"Do you get a snack every time you go on the playground?" Ms. Root asked him.

"Oh . . . I guess not . . ." he said, trailing off. "It might not be good for Cottonball."

"I have a suggestion," said Ms. Root. "Instead of a snack, maybe you could give her something to chew. Hamsters need to chew things to make sure their teeth don't grow too big."

But couldn't Cottonball do her chewing someplace else? Stanley wondered.

"Um, okay, thanks," Stanley said. It was hard to tell a teacher he did not like her idea.

Luckily, in spite of everything, Marco had his back!

Marco looked at Stanley and shook his head. He did not like the idea, either. And he was not afraid to say so.

Marco said, "Ms. Root, I think the obstacle course needs to end with something special. Cottonball needs to feel like she is getting a treat. Not like she is brushing her teeth!"

Ms. Root nodded slowly. "We need to be careful that Cottonball does not get too many treats. But I'm sure Stanley can come up with something both healthy and delicious."

Now Stanley was right back where he started. "I'm still not sure what it should be," he said. "Do hamsters like carrots? Or lettuce? Or Cheerios?"

"Stanley, you know what to do," Marco piped up. "You just need to find out what hamsters eat in the wild!"

The boys started laughing, and then they high-fived. Whatever they built, they would always be friends.

The Tunnel

The next morning, Ms. Root clapped her hands three times to get the class's attention. She said, "We have some exciting news today! Our second-grade engineers have something to show us. Join me at the reading rug to see some creations by Stanley and Marco!"

Desks and chairs scraped against the floor as Stanley's classmates got up and walked to the reading rug.

"What do you think they are?" Juniper asked Josie.

"I heard they were playgrounds for the hamster," Evan told them.

Stanley and Marco were already sitting on the reading rug, behind a little curtain Marco made. Stanley's obstacle course was surrounded by cardboard panels. Cottonball would not be able to get past them if she tried to escape. Marco's maze was contained in a big plastic tray that no hamster could climb out of.

When everyone was settled, Ms. Root said, "Now, friends, Cottonball teaches us about animal life every day, just by being in our classroom.

But I did not expect that our study of animals would change so quickly into a study of engineering! Please welcome two fantastic young engineers!"

As soon as she said that, Marco pulled the curtain back.

Stanley was not thinking about science when he built the obstacle course. He did not even plan to be an engineer. But science was what made the seesaw work and the bridge stay strong. He had used engineering to make Cottonball's life better, and now everyone would see how!

"Elena?" asked Ms. Root. "Would you like to take Cottonball out of her cage?"

Elena was gentle and calm with the hamster. She held Cottonball up against her chest while Marco put a small strawberry in his maze. It turned out wild hamsters loved strawberries!

Marco showed Elena where the maze began, then Elena placed Cottonball at the starting line.

"Watch her find her way toward the prize!" Marco announced to the class.

He expected the hamster to sprint down the paths he had built. He expected her to rush toward the berry.

But when Elena put Cottonball in the maze, the hamster kind of walked in the direction of the straw-berry. When a maze wall blocked her way, though, she looked confused. She turned around and went in another direction. Then she blinked. She stopped. She sat.

"Oh no!" said Stevie. "She can't find her way out!"

"Oh no!" said Marco. "It's not working!" A moment ago, he had been super excited about sending the hamster through the maze. Now he just looked sad.

Stanley knew what Ms. Root would say. Marco could keep working on the maze. Eventually it would be just right!

But Stanley wanted it to be just

right *right now*—and he knew how
to do it!

It was something that only Stanley
Lambchop could do! But first he had
to demonstrate his obstacle course.

Ms. Root took Cottonball out of the
maze and petted her. The hamster

did not seem bothered by her time in the maze. She did not seem to notice the whole class was watching her. Hopefully she was ready to play!

"All right, Stanley," said Ms. Root. "Let's see how she likes your project!" She put Cottonball in front of the cardboard panel, and the hamster wandered over to Stanley's hoop right away. She sniffed it and walked the whole way around it. And then she hopped through the hoop!

"Yay!" said Ms. Root. When the kids started clapping. Ms. Root held a finger up. "Let's give a silent cheer!" she suggested, and the class waved their arms wildly. That way their noise did not scare the hamster.

Next, Cottonball wandered over to Stanley's bridge. She nibbled it for a little while, but it was too big to fit in her small mouth. When she finally gave up on chewing, she decided to go for a walk. She seemed surprised when her walk *up* a ramp became a walk *down* a ramp.

When she reached the bottom, she turned around to look at the top again. Did she want to go back? Stanley thought she might. Then, instead, she walked over to the seesaw!

When Cottonball stepped onto one side of the seesaw, Stanley put his finger on the other side, and she went up into the air! It was only a couple of inches, but Stanley thought she seemed happy. He gently lowered her back down, and when he took his finger off, Cottonball stayed in one spot, as if she wanted to go for another ride. So Stanley lifted her up one more time. Then he gave her a bite of berry.

"That is so cool," Josie said. "Great

job, Stanley!" He beamed. People were always telling Josie she did a great job at things. It was nice to get his own turn, for once.

Still, he noticed no one said "Great job!" to Marco. He was probably disappointed in his maze, Stanley thought. And he had worked so hard on it! Luckily, Stanley knew how a friend could help him. A friend— Stanley!—could engineer a solution.

Stanley handed the hamster to Ms. Root. Then he moved over to the edge of the reading rug and lay down. "What are you doing, Stanley?" Sophia asked. With everyone watching, Stanley Lambchop rolled himself into a neat tube.

Evan thought back to the game they had played in math with mystery shapes. "Are you a cylinder?" he asked.

"No," said Stanley.

"I think he's a tube," Juniper said.

"Guess again!" said Stanley. His voice was a little muffled, because his mouth was near the rug.

"A tunnel?" Marco asked, like he was remembering something.

"Yes!" cried Stanley. He rolled to the space between the obstacle course and the maze. Then he positioned himself right between them, like a secret passage for hamsters. "Cotton-ball loves tunnels, right? Maybe this is the way to get her interested in the maze!"

"Good idea!" said Ms. Root. "Let's see what Cottonball thinks!"

She put the hamster down on the obstacle course side of the Stanley tunnel. Stanley could feel Cottonball's paws as she stood near his feet and sniffed. Then, slowly, she walked into the tunnel he made. When she got inside, she picked up speed. Stanley could feel her tiny nails on his legs.

"Remember, friends, hamsters can run for miles in tunnels!" Ms. Root said.

For a few seconds, it was as if Cottonball were a wild hamster herself! She raced through the Stanley tunnel, back and forth, more times than

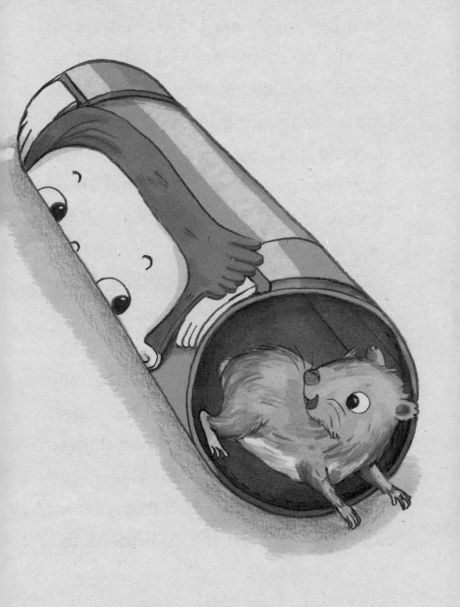

Stanley could count. He tried not to laugh—her footsteps tickled! But he was also wondering the whole time: Is my solution going to work? He hoped that by entering the maze a different way she would be more excited about trying it out. Then she'd have some extra fun!

Pretty soon, it seemed like Cottonball got tired. After one last lap, she left the Stanley tunnel on the maze side. Stanley had made sure that the exit would lead right into the maze. Once she was in there, he stood up to watch with the rest of his class.

This time, Cottonball looked more alert as she went through the maze.

When she came to a wall, she sniffed the air, then changed her path. Was she hungry after her run? Could she tell where the strawberry was? She hit another wall, sniffed again, and circled back. In no time, she got to the end!

"She did it!" Marco said, punching the air.

"Great job, Marco!" Josie said. Even though Stanley had helped a lot.

Ms. Root smiled. "You boys have discovered another rule of engineering," she said. "Sometimes the best solutions come when engineers share ideas."

The best friends looked at each other and smiled. Then, at the same time, they said, "We always do our best work together."

Fun Facts about Hamsters

- Wild hamsters live in dry, open habitats such as plains, dunes, deserts, fields, and more.
- The largest wild hamster is the black-bellied European hamster, which can be up to twelve inches long!
- Hamsters tend to be active at dusk and dawn, and sleep during the day and parts of the night.
- Hamsters have bad eyesight, but they can navigate with their sense of smell and touch—plus their whiskers!

- Hamsters' front teeth grow continuously, and they need to wear them down with items like wood blocks and food.
- Wild hamsters can be aggressive. They will attack animals much bigger than they are!
- Hamsters have cheek pouches that can stretch all the way back to their shoulders. They are used to carry and store food, and even to hide hamster pups.
- Hamsters can run backward as quickly as they can run forward.
- Most hamsters are solitary, which means they do not like to live with other hamsters.